PRAIRIE DAWN, REPORTER

By Linda Hayward
Illustrated by David Prebenna

A SESAME STREET/GOLDEN PRESS BOOK

Published by Western Publishing Company, Inc.,
in conjunction with Children's Television Workshop.

© 1992, 1981 Children's Television Workshop. Sesame Street puppet characters © 1992 Jim Henson Productions, Inc. All rights reserved. Printed in the U.S.A. No part of this book may be reproduced or copied in any form without written permission from the publisher. SESAME STREET®, the SESAME STREET SIGN®, and THE SESAME STREET BOOK CLUB are trademarks and service marks of Children's Television Workshop. All other trademarks are the property of Western Publishing Company, Inc. Library of Congress Catalog Card Number: 80-84526 ISBN: 0-307-23136-4

One morning a big package wrapped in brown paper was delivered to Prairie Dawn.

Inside the package there was a strange-looking machine.

"What can this be?" said Prairie Dawn.

She opened the letter taped to the box.

Dear Prairie,
  When I was a little girl, I printed my own newspaper on this little printing press.
  Now I am giving the printing press to you.
    Hugs and Kisses,
    Aunt Dusk

"I will make a newspaper, too," said Prairie Dawn.

Prairie Dawn took the printing press to her room and set it on the table next to her typewriter.

"What shall I call my newspaper?" she wondered.

"*The Gazette? The Times? The Tribune? The Sun?* That is it! I will call it *The Sesame Street Sun*."

She put on her reporter's hat and her reporter's coat.
She found a pencil and a notebook.
    "Now all I need is some news," said Prairie Dawn.
"That should be easy. I will ask all my friends."

First Prairie Dawn went to the Count's castle.

"Hi!" she said. "I am a reporter for *The Sesame Street Sun*. Do you have any news?"

"Come in, come in," said the Count. "I have five new things in my house. My cat, Ftatateeta, had kittens. Would you like to count them?"

"You may like to *count* kittens," said Prairie Dawn, "but I like to *hold* them."

"What an interesting idea!" cried the Count. "You hold the kittens while I tell you their five fantastic names."

Prairie Dawn wrote the names in her notebook.

Then Prairie Dawn went to Sherlock Hemlock's office. Sherlock Hemlock was busy writing something on a piece of paper.

"Hi, Mr. Hemlock," said Prairie. "I am looking for news for *The Sesame Street Sun*. Are you working on any new cases?"

"Yes, I am," said Sherlock Hemlock. "I am trying to solve The Mystery of the Missing Page. A page of my address book is missing."

His address book was lying on his desk. A page had been torn out of it.

"What are you writing?" asked Prairie.

"This is a list of clues," explained Sherlock Hemlock. "Clue number one—the address book is red. Clue number two—the missing page is blue."

Prairie Dawn looked at the address book. She looked at the list of clues. She wrote something in her notebook.

Then she said, "Congratulations, Mr. Hemlock. I will print in today's paper that you have solved The Mystery of the Missing Page."

"I have? I shall certainly be interested to read your story," replied Sherlock Hemlock, looking puzzled.

Prairie Dawn's next stop was Big Bird's nest.
Big Bird had exciting news.
"Granny Bird has invited me to visit her," he said.
Prairie looked in Big Bird's suitcase.
"Gee, Big Bird," she gasped, "you sure are taking a
lot of stuff. Are you going to stay for a month?"
"No," replied Big Bird, "just overnight."
Prairie Dawn wrote down everything that Big Bird
was taking to Granny Bird's house.

A little farther down the block she met Bert. He had news, too.

"Look at my new collection," he said. "It's my best collection yet."

"What could be better than your bottle cap, eraser, paper clip, and brick collections?" asked Prairie Dawn. She looked into one of the shoe boxes Bert was carrying. Then she looked inside the other three shoe boxes.

"Hmmm. Very interesting," she murmured, as she wrote down the name of Bert's new collection in her notebook.

Then Prairie Dawn went to see The Amazing Mumford. "I have a lot of interesting news for my newspaper," she told him, "but I do not have any really amazing news."

"I will make some amazing news for you," said The Amazing Mumford. "Watch this!"

He waved his magic wand. "A LA PEANUT BUTTER SANDWICHES!" Nothing happened.

"Oh, well," said Prairie Dawn, "I guess I just will not have any amazing news in my newspaper. Thanks anyway, Mr. Mumford." And she started off for home.

Suddenly one hundred and twenty-eight peanut butter sandwiches fell out of the sky and landed all around The Amazing Mumford!

"Come back, Prairie Dawn," called Mumford. "Here is some amazing news for your newspaper."

But Prairie Dawn did not hear him.

As she was passing 123 Sesame Street, Prairie Dawn
met Betty Lou.

"Prairie," said Betty Lou, "where are you going?"

"Home," replied Prairie Dawn. "I have collected lots
of news for my newspaper, and now I am going to write
it up and print it on the printing press my Aunt Dusk
sent me."

"May I help?" asked Betty Lou.

Just then Oscar the Grouch stuck his head out of his can.

"You want news? I have some really big news for you," he said.

"What is it, Oscar?" asked Prairie Dawn. "Is the circus coming to Sesame Street? Is Hooper's Store giving away free apples? Did you find some buried treasure?"

"No, it is none of those things," said Oscar. "I will write it down and bring it to you."

On their way home, Prairie and Betty Lou met Cookie Monster. As soon as he found out about the newspaper, he wanted to help, too.

"Okay," said Prairie Dawn. "Our newspaper needs a food column, and you are just the one to write it. Be sure to deliver your story to my office by our three o'clock deadline."

"You can count on Cookie," said Cookie Monster.

By the time Prairie Dawn and Betty Lou got to Prairie's house, it was lunchtime.

"There is no time to fix lunch, or we will miss our deadline," said Prairie Dawn. "I will call Nelly's Deli.

"Can you deliver two peanut butter sandwiches?" she asked.

"We are all out of peanut butter sandwiches," said Nelly. "How about two egg salad sandwiches?"

"Great!" said Prairie Dawn.

Then Oscar delivered a story about the Annual Grouch Get-Together.

Cookie Monster delivered a review of his favorite cookies.

Nelly's Deli sent over two egg salad sandwiches and a notice for the newspaper's Lost and Found column.

Prairie Dawn and Betty Lou worked all afternoon. By three o'clock all the news stories were ready.

Then Prairie Dawn and Betty Lou found all the letters of the alphabet that spelled all the words that were in all the stories and put them into place on the printing press. This was very hard work.

Next they put ink all over the roller.

Then Betty Lou turned the handle while Prairie
sent a piece of paper through the printing press. It
was exciting to see the printed paper come out.

When they had printed all the newspapers, Prairie Dawn and Betty Lou gave a copy of *The Sesame Street Sun* to everyone on Sesame Street.

And here is a copy for you!

THE SESAME STREET SUN

COUNT'S CAT HAS KITTENS

Ftatateeta, the Count's cat, has five new kittens. They are all adorable. Their names are Fata, Tata, Tati, Tita, and Orange Marmalade.

MYSTERY OF MISSING PAGE SOLVED

A blue page from Sherlock Hemlock's address book mysteriously disappeared today. But the world-famous detective, who lives on Sesame Street, soon solved the case. Mr. Hemlock found the missing page as he wrote his list of clues on it.

BIG BIRD PACKS HIS SUITCASE

Big Bird is going to visit Granny Bird. In his suitcase he is taking his pajamas, a toothbrush, his book of bedtime stories, his book of bird lullabies, his teddy bear, his pillow, his special pillowcase, his snuggly blanket, his very own night-light, his recording of "Nighty-Night Nestling," and a glass of water.

BERT'S NEW COLLECTION

Bert is now collecting shoe boxes. So far he has four shoe boxes in his new collection. "Shoe boxes are really neat," says Bert.

THE GROUCH NEWS
By OSCAR T. GROUCH

The Annual Grouch Get-Together was held at the Dump last week. Delicious sardine sandwiches and ice cold pickle juice were available. It was the best grouch party ever! Nobody came.

LOST!

Today 128 peanut butter sandwiches disappeared, as if by magic, from Nelly's Deli. Anyone who knows anything about this, call Nelly, 123-321.

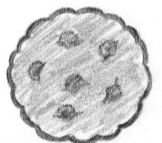

COOKIE REVIEWS

Big Newtons—good
Ginger Crispies—better
Marshmallow Supremes—best
COOOOKIE!

Editor in Chief: PRAIRIE DAWN
Printer: BETTY LOU